# Avi
### the Ambulance
# to the Rescue!

by Claudia Carlson • illustrations by CB Decker

This **PJ BOOK** belongs to

_____

_____

PJ Library®

JEWISH BEDTIME STORIES and SONGS

APPLES & HONEY PRESS

Dedicated to the children who read *Avi* and offered advice:
Max, Owen, and Hayden Carlson; Tristan Mathes; Avi and Jonah Monaco; Ringo and Cody Racheff;
and Leah Michelle Schutz.—CC

To my husband, Morris, who rescues me every day.
—CBD

Apples & Honey Press
An imprint of Behrman House
Behrman House, 11 Edison Place, Springfield, New Jersey 07081
Gefen Publishing House Ltd., 6 Hatzvi Street, Jerusalem, 94386, Israel
www.applesandhoneypress.com

The publisher gratefully acknowledges the following sources of photographs, p. 32: Shutterstock: bandages, photolinc; thank you, bahri altay; mask, Levent Konuk; hands, Triff; veterinarian, wavebreakmedia. All other photos used by permission of Magen David Adom.

Library of Congress Cataloging-in-Publication Data

Carlson, Claudia.
Avi the Ambulance to the rescue! / by Claudia Carlson.
pages cm
Summary: Bored with delivering supplies, Avi the Ambulance wants to rescue someone. Includes author's note on Magen David Adom, Israel's ambulance, blood-services, and disaster-relief organization.
ISBN 978-1-68115-512-8
[1. Ambulances--Fiction. 2. Assistance in emergencies--Fiction. 3. Rescue work--Fiction. 4. Jews--Israel--Fiction. 5. Israel--Fiction.] I. Title.
PZ7.1.C4Aw 2016
[E]--dc23
2015020060
Design by David Neuhaus
Edited by Ann D. Koffsky
Printed in China

041927.8K1/B1377/A4

In a garage in Jerusalem lived a family of ambulances.
Avi was one of the youngest.

Avi's alarm clock buzzed: *Zing-zing-zing.*

"Hurry up, sleepyhead," said his big sister, Maya.
"You can't take hurt or sick people to the hospital
if you're in dreamland!"

Avi's friend, Zack the medic, came to the garage. He and Avi were a team.

Then Maya's medic, Leah, arrived.

They all had breakfast together. Maya told a joke.

Just then, there was a call from headquarters: *Ring! Ring!*

"Maya, someone's been hurt," said Leah. "Let's go!"

*Ring! Ring!*
Moti the Medicycle dashed away.

*Ring! Ring!*
Hila the Helicopter lifted off.

Avi stamped his tires and ground his gears.
"I wish they had called ME to help too!"

"I have a way for you to help," said Avi's mother. "Please check the supplies, and make sure there are enough for all the vehicles."

Zack opened their red bag to check.
He didn't see any water bottles
or bandages.

Avi didn't find any on the supply shelves.

"Ima, we're all out of water bottles and bandages!" said Avi.

"OK. Please go and get more from headquarters," said Avi's mother.

"But I want to help people. Getting supplies is boring," said Avi.

"Avi, you know that water and bandages are important!"

"Cheer up, Avi! Getting supplies won't be so bad if we do it together. Let's get ready to go," said Zack. Zack checked Avi's tires.

Avi checked Zack's shoes. "We're ready," said Avi.

They drove to headquarters, and Zack filled Avi with bandages and water bottles.

Full of boxes, they headed back to the station. Avi huffed and puffed going up the tall Jerusalem hills.

"These boxes are heavy," said Avi. He was so hot that steam came out of his nose.

"Let's stop and rest. I need to drink some of the water we got and cool down," said Avi.

"Me too. Let's watch those kids play soccer," said Zack.

"Good moves," said Zack.
"Can we play too?" asked Avi.

The ambulance reads: MAGEN DAVID ADOM IN ISRAEL מגן דוד אדום בישראל

"Sure!" said Ruthie.
"Playing with an ambulance is fun!"
agreed Isaac.

Suddenly, there was a loud noise:
*Screech, screech, screech!*

"Ima, what happened?" asked Ruthie.
"I made popcorn in the microwave,
and it started to smoke," she answered.
"It set off the smoke detector!"

"Looks like everyone left the building, just to be safe," said Zack.
"Wait!" shouted Ruthie.
"There's still someone inside!" said Isaac.

"It's Yofi!" shouted Ruthie.
"Where?" asked Zack.
Avi turned on his spotlight. "There she is," he said.
"The alarm must have scared her! She's about
to jump!"

Avi drove right under the window.

Yofi jumped from the window, right onto Avi's roof.
Then she jumped again, landing safely on the ground.

Yofi started to cough.

"She must have breathed in some popcorn smoke," said Avi. "Zack, please give Yofi some oxygen to help her breathe."

Zack put an oxygen mask over the cat's nose and mouth.

Yofi opened her eyes and mewed.

"Oh, poor kitty," said Ruthie.

"Yofi-Tofi, you're a good cat," said Isaac. "We love you."

"Is she going to be OK?" asked Ruthie.

"Yes, she'll be just fine," said Zack. "Just make sure she has plenty of water to drink."

"We will," Ruthie and Isaac promised.

By that time, a firefighter arrived in her red truck and parked next to Avi. She entered the apartment building. After a long wait, the firefighter came back out and called, "All clear! It's safe for everyone to come back inside!"

Everyone started to walk back into the building, and Avi and Zack began their drive to the garage with the boxes of bandages and water.

That night in the garage the ambulances and medics celebrated the helpful work they had done that day. Maya and Leah told everyone how they took people to the hospital.

"Avi and I brought supplies to the station," said Zack.

"That was a big help," said Avi's mother.

" And we helped Yofi the cat!" said Avi.

"That's great, Avi. We all work to help everyone, big or small," said Maya.

"Or furry!" Avi added. Everyone laughed.

The next day, Avi and Zack drove back to visit Yofi.
Yofi brushed against Avi's hood. Avi fed Yofi a can
of tuna. And Yofi purred and purred.

# The Lifesaving Work of Magen David Adom

The story of Avi is based on the real work of Magen David Adom (MDA), Israel's ambulance, blood-services, and disaster-relief organization, whose emergency medical first responders serve the country's more than 8 million people.

*Avi the Ambulance to the Rescue!* shows how Jewish values are observed, learned, and applied: *piku'ach nefesh*, the importance of saving lives; *tza'ar ba'alei chayyim*, caring for animals; and *hakarat hatov*, expressing appreciation to others for their help.

More than fourteen thousand professionals and volunteers help save lives at MDA. You can learn more at www.afmda.org.

**Ambulance**

**Mobile Intensive Care Unit (MICU)**

**Bloodmobile**

**Helicopter**

**Command Car**

**Medicycle**

Can you match the characters in the story to the photos on this page?

## Vocabulary

**ambulance:** A special truck used to move hurt or sick people to a hospital. The ambulance has medical supplies inside. Avi is an ambulance.

**bandage:** A piece of material used to protect a hurt part of the body.

*hakarat hatov:* Expressing appreciation to others.

*ima:* "Mommy" or "mother," in Hebrew.

**medic:** A person trained to help take care of hurt or sick people. Zack and Leah are medics.

**medical helicopter:** A special helicopter used to quickly move hurt or sick people to a hospital. The helicopter has medical supplies inside. Hila is a medical helicopter.

**medicycle:** A motorcycle used to reach and help sick and hurt people fast, until an ambulance can get there. Moti is a medicycle.

**mobile intensive care unit (MICU):** A bigger ambulance that has more medical supplies to take care of people who are very hurt or sick. Maya is a MICU.

**oxygen mask**: A mask that is placed over the nose and mouth to supply a patient with additional oxygen to breathe.

**paramedic bag:** A bag that a medic uses to carry supplies.

*piku'ach nefesh*: The Jewish value of saving a life, so important that it supersedes virtually every other commandment.

*tza'ar ba'alei chayyim*: The Jewish value of caring for animals and treating them humanely.

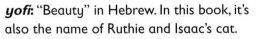

*yofi*: "Beauty" in Hebrew. In this book, it's also the name of Ruthie and Isaac's cat.